William John Lynd

Brantley

A Drama in Five Acts

William John Lynd

Brantley
A Drama in Five Acts

ISBN/EAN: 9783337343477

Printed in Europe, USA, Canada, Australia, Japan

Cover: Foto ©Andreas Hilbeck / pixelio.de

More available books at **www.hansebooks.com**

—A—

Drama in Five Acts.

—BY—

WILLIAM JOHN LYND.

DRAMATIS PERSONÆ.

BRANTLEY..*A Minister.*

J. CONWELL,
TIM RILEY, } ....*Miners.*
DICK LAWSON,

PAT SYMES.....................................*Gardener and Miner.*

OBERHEIM..*A Bishop.*

KOOGLAND.............................*A Swedish Gentleman.*

FITZ HUGH....................................*An English Lord.*

ANTONICELLI.............................*A Catholic Priest.*

DON SEBASTIANO, } ....*Spanish Dons.*
DON GOMEZ,

KOOGLAND'S FATHER ....

MISS CHADWELL.....................*A young lady of wealth.*

MRS. PERCY.........................*Aunt of Miss Chadwell.*

MISS RUSSELL, } *Young lady friends of Mrs. Percy and Miss*
MISS TRAVERS, *Chadwell.*
MISS FLORENCE,

MAUD..*A Gipsy Queen.*

OLD JOE, *and* GRANNY, *and* YOUNG JOE,
Stewarts, Pages, and others.

GOLDEN, COL.:
PRINTED BY GEORGE WEST, TRANSCRIPT OFFICE.
1876.

ACT I.

Scene I. *Louisiana. Parlor in Mrs. Percy's mansion.*

Koogland *and* Miss Chadwell *playing at chess.*

Koog. Oft times, so history declares to us,
Our fates depend upon a game like this.
Though science did the victory achieve,
An unforseen disaster yet may snatch
The prize, and sink my triumph in defeat.

Miss C. It would be well to win your laurels first ;
The sunrise see, before you weep the sunset.

Koog. That unexpected move! another such,
And all my practiced skill avails me not.
And yet it would uncourteous be to take
Success within my grasp : defeat to suffer,
Though able to prevent it, this should be my part.

Miss C. Be on your guard ; defeat approaches swiftly.
Forget your gallantry, and try your utmost.

Enter Brantley.

Bran. To-night the stars throw out their keenest
lustre,
Like diamonds of different water set
In lucid azure glass, at distances,
That give unto the whole an untold glory,
And lend to every one a higher beauty.

Miss C. The stars, I've often heard, do rule our fates,
As Jupiter, or other favoring orbs
Are in ascendant. Which now sways the hour ?
This game is lost, or won, as it ordains.

Bran. There's one o'ertops the rest, the planet Venus.
But pallid Saturn looks malevolent.
To prove his aspect, let me end this battle.

Miss CHADWELL *surrenders her place and looks on.*

Miss C. Take care you lose not the advantage gained.

Koog. A fitting warning to the side you favor.
The stars now fight against your Sisera ;
The victory is mine.

Miss C. Old Saturn bears
'Gainst you a grudge ; you scarcely guessed the power
Of his malevolence. In starry groupings
The beauteous Venus does not always rule.

Bran. I hoped his heart, surcharged with passions dark,
Would yield somewhat to her enchanting smiles.

Miss C. Converging aspects you perhaps confounded,
And so another's lot believed your own.

Bran. Perchance I did. If so I must resign
Myself to Heaven's mysterious decrees.
Each destiny is writ by the same hand,
That poised the silent brilliants in yon sky,
Their mystic language formed, and story shaped,
The gemmed scroll, that in its mazy change,
Foretells unerringly the solemn future.
I go to read my fate, and bid adieu. [*Exit.*

Koog. The influence benign that rules the hour
(*Kneels.*) Constrains a full confession of my love
And heart's devotion, and that here's the shrine
Of my idolatry. To thee, Miss Chadwell,
I turn always ; for thee I live ; and none
Else shall e'er swerve from thee my loyal heart—

Miss C. (*Rising.*) Desist, sir, I entreat you. This surprises me.
Bestow elsewhere your loyalty, and worship ;
On me they will be lost. Good night !

Koog. (*Rising.*) Stay ! stay !
If love thou canst not give, then give me friendship.
I ask, implore you be my friend.

Miss C. So be it.
But not again beyond that barrier pass. [*Exit.*

Koog. She's gone ! and must my love e'en thus subside ?
Cold friendship ! oh can such repose o'ertake
The mad'ning heavings of this bursting heart !
No ! never ! no ! as wildly surged the waters
Above the highest peaks, and all around

Were clouds and darkness, thus is my soul.
No rainbow can ever span its heaven.   [*Exit.*
(w.)

SCENE 2.—*Part of a conservatory at Mrs. Percy's.*
Enter TIM RILEY *arranging a bouquet, and then* PAT
SYMES *carrying a tray with flower cuttings.*

Symes. Here I am with the tray and flowers. Such
jewels of flowers! the belles of the conservatory, as rare
as ostriches in old Tipperary. Do ye mind. They
would put a blush on the diamonds in the queen's crown,
and make a duchess forget her beauty. Do ye mind.
It is a sin to destroy the life of these poor swate inno-
cents for that puffed up roll of church pastry. Do ye
mind.

Riley. It is a sin, Pat, but how can we help it. The
pursy, oyster-fed, wine-aromatized, sleek-tongued bishop, will dive his nose like a humming bird into every
flower, and run his gray eye over every leaf and bud of
this bouquet.

Symes. You may well say that. Do ye mind. He'll
search the floral dictionary to see the emblims, so he
will. This she put there to mane esteem, that she ar-
ranged close by to denote warm affection, and that to
tell of hope, and that to expect the wedding day.

Riley. The old bishop has a keen eye to worldly pelf.

Symes. That's true, Tim. The sheep that carries the
most wool holds the eye of the big shepherd, and feels
the gentle love-taps of his crozier. Do ye mind. Or as
the old proverb has it, the cock clucks most to the
fattest hen.

Riley. What a royal palace will he have, and in what
a sumptuous carriage will he roll his bulky frame,
should he marry our lady.

Symes. St. Peter and St. Paul, *pax vobiscum!* St.
Peter who holds the kays of heaven never strained steel
springs, nor rolled on carriage cushions. Do ye mind.
St. Peter, who thought like a sage, but felt like a man,
with all his illigance, never had such a bouquet as that to
timpt him. He was too busy, as Tim Flannigan used
to say, when he hunted the fleas on his old toothless
dog, to attind to such vanities. Do ye mind.

Riley. Madame Percy is too sensible to fall into the
cunning trap of that fleshly round of godly pretence.

Symes. I crossed the Atlantic ocean. Do ye mind.
All ships do not sail into port. The eagle does not always catch his fish.

Riley. That's so, Pat. Leeches curl into balls, and dart around, and then elongate into miniature sea serpents, and glide about with all the curves of beauty, but fail to fasten on to their victims.

Symes. I am not a prophet, Tim, but do ye mind, I see breakers ahead. The devil's snuff-box will sink in sight of dry land.

Riley. I think you a true prophet, Pat. Now, when you carry this *handing him the boquet)* breathe a little malice on it as you go, and pray that his courtship may prove a sunken ship, that his strapping leg may become a cork leg, and his twanging nose a dividing ridge to serve as a water shed for his swelling tears, when disappointment leers at his fallen hopes.

Symes. Do ye mind. I will put such a spell round this bunch of roses, that he will have to doctor his divinity, and turn apothecary to his soul.

Riley. Ha! ha! ha! Meet me in the garden at the lower end, and let me know how he smiled, and how he said, bless me, as he held it up, what a gem! what a condensation of beauty! My thanks to your mistress.

Symes. Do ye mind. Sure as big whales eat little fish, I will note every twinkle of his eye, every curl of his lip, and every tone of his voice, and will bring back an overflowing fund for a week's laughter. Do ye mind.
(w.)   [*Exeunt—both laughing.*

SCENE 3.—*Louisiana. A garden at Bishop Oberheim's.*

Enter Mrs. PERCY *and Bishop* OBERHEIM.

Mrs. Percy. The Swede, so rumor states, soon sails
       for Europe.
With him rebuffs in love are hard to bear ;
His passion's fierce, and burns his life away.
'Tis pity one so rich, and comely too,
With noble talents, and high family,
Should feel the pangs of unrequited love.
My niece is wilful, needs a stronger will
To govern, and control her moods, and fancies.

Bp. Ob. True wisdom counsels caution, and suggests,
That other cause than wilfulness exists.

My serving man last week espied the cause.
He saw pass out the garden gate young Brantley
With face upturned, and gazing at the stars.
"Now all is well," he said, "I see defeat
Will follow my competitor this night."
Behind a tree the faithful spy now hid,
And watched till Brantley was full out of sight ;
Then suddenly there dashes forth a steed
All shining black, the rider urging him ;
All crazed he flew, like as a very demon.
This was the Swede. Let us remove the cause ;
Send Brantley far away ; and soon your niece
Will good advice and counsel heed.

    Mrs. P. Your wise sagacity I much commend.

    Bp. Ob. To-morrow Brantley's aspirations fall.
He'll find the tender roots of daring love,
By sharp authority both cut and severed.
His soul a wreck will learn humility.

    Mrs. P. My thanks, good Bishop, for this welcome
      help.
My niece's time I'll occupy with visits, balls,
Soirees, receptions Wary spies will watch her.
We'll travel, and no contrivance be witheld
To wither, and consume this ill-timed fancy.
Adieu.   [*Exit.*

    Bp. Ob. Farwell, may heaven bless your work.
Here Brantley comes. To-day, and not to-morrow.
I will the blow, that crushes him, let fall
His face is radiant with smiles.

          Enter BRANTLEY.

    Bran.   I hope
Your grace is well. This glorious day excites
My blood. Olympian airs could not enthuse
One's spirits more. My soul is jubilant ;
The birds' songs, the fountain's gleams, and hum of
    bees,
In sweet accord do thrill my heart.

    Bp. Ob.   'Tis said
The days on Afric's coast are always such.
Perhaps you would prefer their steady warmth
To changeful climes like this. An urgent call
For laborers in that pleasant field seeks you.
It comes most seasonably too. This church

Requires more age, experience, and rare power.
For zeal, devotion to the poor, pure life,
High stands your record. This call weigh well.
Your wishes bring to-night. So now good day. [*Exit.*
   Bran. Another turn in destiny. This morn
The sea of life was joyous, and its waves
Beneath the sunbeams danced innumerous.
But my horizon now's a line of darkness;
Clouds rise, and tempests swell the angry billows.
The stars told me not this. To trust in them
How vain! But oh,—must I go hence and leave thee
Miss Chadwell? No! oh, no! I feel thou lovest me.
This anchors my frail bark. I'll meet the storm.
Upon my knees, nay prostrate, I will call
To him who rules the furious elements.
Oh, Jesus! Master! help, teach me to pray.
   (*Ring Slow Drop.*)

ACT II.

Scene 1.—*Miners' Cabin in Rocky Mountains.*

Jonas Conwell, Dick Lawson, Tim Riley, *Miners.*

   Conwell. The early snows compel a quick descent
To parks, plains, and more temperate altitudes.
But while the summer lasts, no region smiles
Like this in all the world. The rivers hence
That flow, on either side, to ocean slopes,
The tributes, which turn wheels of industry,
And gladden ruddy toil with smiling harvests,
To populations large, and far convey,
And rival fertile Nile, and sacred Ganges.
Right on the brink of melting snows do glow
In sweetest freshness, flowers of every hue;
While in the dashing waterfalls whose drops,
Like coruscating gems, flash out their beauty,
Glides round the wary fish. Here, too, the eye
Surveys the multitudinous crested peaks
Like hillocks lessening in the distance; while
At night each star throws out its vivid colors,
And sailing meteors, as they pass, shed radiance

Upon the still and snow-clad slumbering summits.
Here I can pray without a rosary.

Tim R. And so can I, my friend, but born and bred
A Catholic, 'tis hard to break the spell
Of habit. Organ tones will fill the ear;
I see the vested priest, and acolytes
Waving the incense, while the kneeling crowd
Bow to the adored host. At times I see
With all its pomp, the great St. Peter's Church,
Where sits the Pope who sways our faith, and hopes.

Con. That architectural fane, and wonder, nought
Is to the temple we might build. The gems
And metals lying in these rocky beds,
Could rear a sacred pile of heavenly splendor;
Its walls all silver, pillars, roof all gold;
Topazes, agates, garnets, emeralds, rubies,
Round altar, shrines, and all the dome,
Enough to dazzle, and amaze an angel.

Lawson. The precious stones recall to mind, a good
And pious minister, who taught the Word
Divine, its inner sense with skill unfolding.
Sermons from stones, and trees, and clouds he gave.
You doubtless knew him, Conwell, for he held
The key to heavenly truth. And as with ease
You can unlock its secrets too, it seems
That you must know him.

Con. Yes, indeed, I do.
Through him I learned the Word's interior sense.
(*A noise from a snow slide.*) But hark!

Tim. R. It is an avalanche. My ears
Do not deceive me.

Law. Come! now all is still,
Let us go out and see. [*Exeunt and return.*

Tim. That mass of snow
Had it a little larger been, had given
To all of us an inner sense. Friend Conwell,
Expound this miracle, this escape from death.

Con. The falling of the snow, its loosening,
And its descent, huge boulders sweeping
And giant trees confused, down its broad path,
Are nature's laws; but we so ruled by Him
Without whose will a sparrow falleth not,

2

That now we live, and can his praise proclaim.
This cabin stands untouched, and still our home,
And not our grave, because Divine foresight
And loving kindness moved us here to build
Beyond destruction's verge.

  Tim.   You reason well.
This Providence agrees with nature's laws.
Our safety hangs on spirit influence.

  Con. Friend Tim, you're quick to comprehend.
Another truth receive. The Lord incarnate
Walking this earth, shone like the rising sun,
Yea brighter than the noon-day sun he shone,
But through the interior atmosphere ; and so
The natural eye could not behold the glory.
The lake Gennesaret was smooth, and all
The air was still ; the Master in deep sleep
Reposing on a pillow, when the wind
Suddenly caught the sails, and heaped the waves
In higher and higher swelling, might and foam,
Until the ship that bore him nearly sank.
Then fearful hands aroused him. He rose
And threw a glance upon the demon throng
That raised the storm. That glance they saw, and heard
Distinctly, "Peace be still," and fled in pain.
The air and sea resumed their wonted calm.

  (*Two tourists appear at window.*)
  Tim. That's true.
  1st Tourist. We have found a snug harbor.
  Tim. They are the powers that occupy—
  2d Tourist. Just in time for warm cheer.
  Tim The subtler parts of nature. So again
'Twas spirit on spirit moving lulled the storm.

  Con. 'Twas even so, Tim.

     Enter two TOURISTS *with guns.*

  1st. Tour.   We are bold to enter ;
For doors here have no barring locks, or bolts.
And all are welcome.

  Tim.   True, put down your guns.
Your looks are jaded. Seat yourselves and rest. [TIM
  gives stools.] We'll sup ere long.

   [LAWSON *gets supper ready ;* CONWELL *and* TIM *listen*
   to tourists.

2d Tour.   We both are hungry men.
Our appetites are sharpened by a fast
Of two whole days. A driving snow compelled
Us shivering, to seek a hiding place
Upon the mountains yonder. With much effort
A tree was fired. The blazing pine soon carved
An opening round its trunk ; in this we dropped
And so escaped the blast. The crackling flames
Despite the falling flakes shot up from branch
To branch. The veil of snow, the leaping fires
We watched, till flickering in taper light,
Our mountan lamp went out, and darkness reigned.
In our snow cell thus cooped, we passed the time,
Until we had an icy floor o'er which
Quite weak we slowly reached this sheltering roof.

   1st. Tour. As we approached we saw the thundering
     slide
That near o'erwhelmed your home. Our cheeks were
     blanched.
Our hearts stood still. Had you been buried here,
We too, had perished. The curlews's whistling flight,
In this high atmosphere, would not again
Disturb our listless ears. Some playful bear
Perchance had pulled this trigger, turned about
And fled precipitate, alarmed at flash
And sound. Perchance the queenly lioness
In joyous gambols with her cubs had rolled
All heedless of our whitened bones. Or deer
With antlers proud had bounded in full spring
Right o'er the remnants of our once strong frames
In breathless haste, and distancing pursuit.
The hand that saved you, saved us. Let us sing
A hymn of praise.
                  [The two tourists sing.

CHORUS.
Come, come comfort me
In the time of need.

1. Our angel guards defend us,
   In every moment, every hour ;
Through mountain storms they tend us,
   'Mid ocean's rage, we feel their power.
                  Come, come &c.

2. O, Lord, our life thou holdest,
   While naught escapes thy watchful care ;
The powers of hell, when boldest,
   Can touch us not, nor harm a hair.

                              Come, come &c.

Con. The Albigenses, pious mountaineers,
Could not pour out their thanks more fervently.
Friends, let me clasp your hands, embrace you, too.
The Lord is in your hearts, your eyes are opened,
You are not strangers to the word of truth.

   Tim. Why do such trustful men such weapons bear?

   1st. Tour. We carry arms not for defence, but food.
'Tis strange how we came here.   Two months ago,
My friend and I were walking arm in arm
O'er gravelled walks, beneath the shade of tall
And aged elms, and maples, viewing all
The landscape.   Towering there the mountains high,
Changeful through moving lights, and shadows seemed ;
While winding round the smooth shorn lawn, a stream
Through openings broad, flashed back the sun,
And clustering trees, at proper intervals
Along the banks, the watery view concealed.
We talked of Alpine snows, and frozen heights
Where all is mute and solitary calm.
That day a letter came inviting us
To visit this our Switzerland.   At once
With youthful ardor we set out.   We had
One other with us, Charles Brantley.

   Con.   Where is he?
Oh! oh, that I might meet him once again!

   1st. Tour. You know him too?   On yon white man-
      tled peak
That Sphinx-like looks down on far stretching plains,
And eyes the snow-fed Platte in its strange turns,
Keeps silent watch on busy towns, on toils
Of husbandry, and feeding flocks, and herds,
We left him.

   Con.   On Long's peak? Is he so near?

Knocking at door enter BRANTLEY.

   Con. Friend Brantley! this surprise o'ercomes me
      quite.

Bran. I'm glad to see you Conwell. Who are these?
Why, Harris, Bush and—
    Tim.   Tim and Dick.
We all rejoice to meet you here. How did
You find us thus? What hither turned your feet?
    Bran. Constrained by secret power, my friends I left
To go in quest of these. A furious storm
O'ertook my steps in yonder gulch. A sort
Of cave, or tunnel gave me timely shelter.
In holy thought the hours flew swiftly by.
I thought of Chimborazo's swelling dome
Of dazzling white far up the cloudless blue
Of heaven upreared. Volcanoes breathing fire ;
For ages then, in death-like torpor lying.
How down the sunlit craters bloomed the rose,
And fragrant shrubs, in leafy foliage,
The desolation hid ; while far above
In the blue vault, the condor soared and sailed
With outspread wings. Thus life, I thought, death fol-
    lows,
And scatters over his dark path all sweet
Benignities. I then recalled the scenes
Which toilsome steps revealed on yonder peak—
The *Key*, that curious rock, cut in such shape
As just to fit the wards of some huge lock
Of Nature; and the cold wierd stillness there,
As the round moon rose up above the clouds
That wide encanopied the plains, and hung
Adown the mountain's side ; those moving vapors
That far below like waves of ocean seemed,
While to the ear the sound of dashing torrents
All hid from view, and fed by melting snows,
Came as old ocean's steady beat of waves
Upon the shore. Thus thought succeeded thought,
Till on the eastern verge of vision leaped
The reddening tints of dawn. The ruddy light
To kiss the peak's white chilly brow then flew,
Imprinting pure sweet rosy blushes there.
The world seemed then as if new born ; and each
Clear crystalled flake threw back the salutation,
All like a million prisms. I felt the thrill
Of this empurpling glory. Adoration

Seized me. I knelt and humbly blessed our God.
Snug housed in my retreat, I passed the night; [*Lawson and Tim place table and chairs.*

Next morn essayed the snow compact and frozen ;
It bore my weight, and weary here I am.

   Con. You're hungry too, dear friend.

   Dick Lawson.   The supper's ready.

[*All sit down at table but Lawson who waits, Brantley
in attitude of prayer.*

(w.)

   SCENE 2.—*Spain.—Street in Granada.*

   Enter grooms of rival Dons of Granada.

   1st. *Groom.* Since that American lady of beauty, and
wealth came to town I have no rest. Up early and late,
and kept on the full stretch. I have absolutely no time
to play the lute under my true love's window—no time.

   2d *Groom.* The bear that always sleeps gives weak
hugs. The idle mill-wheel soon falls to pieces. Vessels
that lie still in harbor have most barnacles. The bark
becomes loose on sapless trees.

   1st. *Groom.* Hush! no more proverbs. You have
no pity for my helpless lot. You can troll your song to
her you love these moonlight nights.

   2d *Groom* Too much knowledge brings sorrow.
Too little begets envy. This very night as soon as the
stars blink through the trees on the hooting owl, and
waken the sweet melodies of the nightingale, and then
stand aloof in ambuscade, while a few, here and there,
appear as silent watchers behind the queenly moon,
sparks will fly from steeled hoofs dashing with my Señ-
or to the Alhambra.

   1st. *Groom.* Is he too, smitten with the fair charmer?

   2d *Groom.* Mælstroms draw down ships. Water-
spouts draw up water. The moon draws the ocean.
All things are under attraction. My Señor will play
the lute and sing under that lady's window to-night.

   1st. *Groom.* To-night? Will he sing one of your
songs?

   2d *Groom.* Yes, and set to one of your airs.

   1st. *Groom.* That gives me a bright idea. You can
compose poetry better than I, and I can compose music
better than you. Let us form a joint company.

2d Groom. Agreed. You will sing my verses, and I will play your music. Its a bargain. (*They join hands*)

From right enter FELICIA, *1st. groom's sweetheart, coming from market with basket full of vegetables, &c.*

Felicia. So you have made a bargain, haven't you? The way you put your hands together, and your looks tell me so.

1st. Groom. Yes; a curious bargain, too.

Felicia. What is it?

1st. Groom. We have each agreed to personate the other when we play our lute, and sing to our beloved.

Felicia. You won't be able to deceive me.

Enter CATHARINA *from left, 2d groom's sweetheart, going to market.*

Felicia. What do you think? these have both agreed to deceive us, to put on false faces, and disguise their voices, and pass each off for the other.

Cath. Ha! ha! ha! I will put cotton in my ears, and shut my eyes.

Felicia. And I will get my father's fishing rod, hook and line, and catch the false face and pull it off.

[*All laugh.*

Cath. And I will let our big dog Cæsar out, and that will change his tune. "Oh, call him! Call him! It is I." [*All laugh.*

2d Groom. Boiling water relieves no hunger. Young hawks famish without meat. No vegetables, no olla podrida.

1st Groom. If your basket held a thousand things, he'd give a proverb for every one. He strings proverbs as children do peach-stone kernels, or monks, avemarias.

[*Convent bell rings.*

Felicia (startled), That hurries me. Adios. [*Exit.*

2d Groom So the earth by waltzing hurries the sun. Adios.

1st Groom. Adios.

Cath. And me, too. Adios. [*Exit.*

Both grooms. Adios.

1st Groom. We meet to-night.

2d Groom. To-night at moonrise.

1st Groom. Adios.

2d Groom. Adios. [*Exeunt.*

(w)

SCENE 3.—*Spain.—Garden of the Alhambra by moon-light.*

Enter Mrs. PERCY *and* Miss CHADWELL.

Mrs. Percy. The skies of Spain do not improve your
     health.
You do not smile and laugh enough. You seem
A wonder to the Dons of gay Madrid.
Your sparkling wit, your brilliancy have fled,
Why fix your thoughts on that poor friendless youth,
That fou-fou, Brantley? Come, be like yourself.
On your return display your mental wealth ;
Put on your most bewitching charms. In dress,
In grace, in wit, excel. Then princely hearts
Will kneel in meek devotion at your feet.

Miss Chadwell. My own dear aunt, I'll try to do
     your bidding.
Yon moon spreads over all her gauzy veil ;
Each leaf, and flower drinks in the dewy air ;
The beamy stars disclose but half their lustre.
In floral taste, in harmonizing tints
And perfumes, shaping tesselated walks,
And interlacing vines, and trees
Of variant shades, and bearing fruits sweet-scented,
Like tempting Eden, clusters hung just where
The spray of fountains falls in gentle drops,
And blends into the hush of silent night,
The Moors had inspiration from the skies.

Mrs. Percy. See, yonder come the fond and trusting
     twain,
Whose close-bound hearts to each their thoughts reveal.

Enter MISS RUSSELL *and* MISS TRAVERS.

Miss Chadwell. 'Tis sweet to see again this loveliness
When day withdraws his heat, and glaring light.
Look here, Miss Russell. (*Turns and points to a crown
     of growing flowers*).

Mrs. Percy.   Will Miss Travers go
Once more with me to see the Hall of Lions ?

Miss Russell. Do not stay long. Oh, what a beaute-
     ous fancy !
A floral crown ! The roses intertwined
Most gracefully, unsevered from their stems,
The buds, and blooms, with cunning skill commingled.

I would transfer it to thy brow, Miss Chadwell,
To antedate the' angelic coronation
That surely waits for thee in yonder skies.

Miss C. Your loving spirit breathes such sweet perfume
You make me quite forget those blended odors
That here delight the sense. But now a truce
To flattery. You know that gentleman,
That millionaire, whose wealth is drawn from out
The hills, the treasure vaults of Colorado?

Miss Russell. That gentle, quiet, unassuming soul,
Who pours out riches of bright thoughts received
From one of heaven's illumined messengers?
I knew him well. The unseen world he ope'd
To my enraptured eyes, and by his aid
I saw of truth divine, the hidden glories,
The heavenly light.

    Miss C.   Who is that favored seer?

Miss Russell. His name is Brantley. Why so deeply
    blush?
That tell-tale crimson, oh! what does it mean?

    Miss C. A favor grant. Acquaint me with your
    friend.

    Miss Russell. That will I do most gladly. Hark,
    Miss Chadwell!   [*Voice is heard singing.*

    Miss C. And now thy rosy mantled cheek discovers
Some hidden tale. This way the music comes;
The tones how soft and tender.

Enter CONWELL singing

    "Remember thee, and all thy pains,
      And all thy love to me;
    Yes, while a breath, a pulse remains,
      Will I remember thee."

    Con. Your pardon, ladies, I was forced to sing,
The spirit of the place controlled me so.
I sought, and gladly found you here, Miss Russell.

(Miss R. presents Miss C.)

    Miss C. We all are charmed. The night is so inspiring
The birds are loathe their tiny heads to nestle
Beneath their wings. That hymn deep thrilled my
    heart,
Recalling memories dear of church and home.

    Con. Your former pastor breathes Italian air;

3

Charles Brantley's now the seer.   His feet are turned
This way ere this.   He'll soon be in Madrid.
    Miss Russell.   (*To Conwell.*)   You've told too much.
      (*To Miss C.*)   You look confused, Miss Chadwell.
Just let me tell—but hush! here comes your aunt.

    Enter MRS. PERCY *and* MISS TRAVERS.

    Mrs. P.   My niece, 'tis growing late.   Let us return.
Good night.   [*Mrs. P. and Miss C. exeunt.*
    Miss Travers.   Would you believe it, that sagacious
    aunt
Drew me away to talk about you both.
She questioned first as to your wealth and friends;
And then as if to penetrate my soul
She gazed, and said—"spoke he to you of Brantley?"
I hardly murmured "yes" when here she hurried.
    Miss Russell.   Poor girl! to love, and be beloved; to see
Hope's headland come in sight, then clouds, and mists
Hide all from view.   Perhaps she'll leave Granada
Before another dawn.   Her aunt's resolved
That Brantley's hand to hers shall ne'er be joined.
    Miss Travers.   'Tis strange.   How came you on the
    scene just then?
Of you she'll ask her niece, and she, so frank,
So truthful, too, will not prevaricate.
    Con.   Came they without attendants?   I will go—
    Miss Travers.   And leave us here; that will be gal-
    lantry.
Outside the garden walls their carriage stands.
Two rival dons there, on high mettled steeds
That paw the earth impatiently, watch for them
To see them in Granada safely housed.
    Con.   May angels pure attend, and comfort her.
These quick events almost distracted me,
And drew my thoughts away from what surrounds us.
The Moors, in their effulgent cloudless heaven,
Enjoy the finer types, and essences
Of all the floral kingdom.   These reveal
Not e'en a shadow of the vivid colors
Of flowers supernal, nor give forth a breath
Of soul entrancing sweetness such as theirs,
Nor so dissolve in living melody.
There in angelic mansions, floral wreaths

In rich profusion, pillars, chambers, halls,
Encircle, brought and hung by unseen hands;
The wreaths, with tints, and fragrance new enlivened,
Th' angelic thoughts, and loves, and joys depicting,
As they ascend from height to height of bliss.

Miss Travers. The Scriptures call our God as now
    revealed,
The Lily and the Rose.

Con.   As symbols these
Are beautiful, but faintest adumbrations.
But when their source, and essences are known,
Then clearly God through them will be revealed.
As things celestial root themselves in men
New floral types from heaven will then appear,
And fill the world with paradisal sweetness.

Miss Travers. The fauna, too, it seems, must feel the
    new
Creative ordering.

Con.   Yes. Inverted types
Will wholly vanish. Lions round our fountains
Will take their quiet rest, and peace will reign—
But who approaches? 'Tis Don Gomez.

Enter DON GOMEZ.

Don G. A glorious night for a knight-errant's proof
In search of one he worships. Is it not, Miss Travers?

Miss Travers. If Don Quixote like, he bends the
    knee of homage
To objects of imaginary claims,
And vows with ceremonious chivalry,
He is a knight of questionable glory.

Don G. Alas! alas! my ready wit has fled.

Miss Travers. Then call for Sancho quick, he'll bring
    it back.

Don G. In truth, Miss Travers—

Miss Russell.   Rescue! pause a moment.

Con. Things unforseen do sometimes rear and balk
Engagements, though they be most solemn.
I will presume to mediate, and say,
Miss Travers in her heart excuses you.
Just now we talked of all this floral wealth;
And I was on the point of celebrating
Our visit here with improvised song—

Don Gom. Oh yes! give us the song—
Miss R. and Miss T.   The song! the song!
Con. You'll join me in the chorus.   [*sings.*

CHORUS—
         Oh angels come, oh angels come,
         Strew flowers around us here.

1   Home's sacred joys are seen in flowers,
     And thoughts that spring from love,
  That life that's filled with hallowed hours,
     And wisdom from above.
                              Chorus.

2   The floral blooms, on spirit earths,
     The angels' love display,
  And truths, in new unfolding births,
     That form the heavenly day.
                              Chorus.

3   The floral life, in angel lands,
     The love of God reveals,
  And truth divine, which always stands,
     And joys forever yields.
                              Chorus.

(*Ring Drop.*)

———◆———

ACT III.

SCENE 1.—*Rome. Chamber of a Priest.*

FATHER ANTONICELLI *reading, rises as* LORD FITZ
HUGH *enters.*

Father A. Good day, my friend! Sent you to Signor
     Brantley?
And will he come?
   Fitz H.   He comes to-day at five.
   Father A. (*Looks at watch.*) He then will soon be
     here. Fitz Hugh, we mortals
To our own choice, and wisdom are not left.
All things do operate, as God ordains
For his dear children in this changeful world.
The ordeals, through which I these weary months
Have passed, are strange, mysterious, and terrible,
And in my soul have pressed the solemn truth

So deep, that Jesus is the Only God,
And that his human is Divine, in Him
The fulness of the Godhead wholly dwells,
That time, nor yet eternity can e'er
Efface it. On this central truth my thoughts
Were fixed, and prayers went up for light, more light.
An influx warm, and cold by turns set in ;
The conscious subject of two moving powers
My soul became. My inner sight was opened
To that degree, short glimpses of th' invisible
Both dark, and light were seen. My agonies
Were fearful, and at last, the Lord Himself
To me was manifest. And now to me
The Human is Divine. This must be true.

(*Servant announces* SIGNOR BRANTLEY.)

Father A. Bid him enter.   [*Enter* BRANTLEY.
Father A. I'm glad that you have come. Through
    lord Fitz Hugh
I learned that consciously in two degrees
Of respiration you exist. That on
This plane the natural, you see, and feel
As we do ; also on the spirit plane
Are cognizant of things to us invisible,
Of what occurs among the blessed angels.
To me short glimpses of the eternal spheres
Have been vouchsafed, as drawn aside, or closed
The curtain parting seen, and unseen worlds.
I would the purport of these visions learn.
    Bran. Jesus our Lord has chosen you a medium
Through which to work his gracious will.
In time you too will be a conscious dweller
At once in this, and in the spirit world.
    Father A. Your views of God, of heaven, of earth,
    of men
Detailed in full to me by lord Fitz Hugh,
While new are most convincing, and uplifting.
I love our planet now ; it is my mother ;
This outer man is mother to the inner ;
Regenerate men the mother of our heavens.
The pulses of new life into this world's
Heart pressing, beat through me in music chimes.
My Master now, I know, all things pervades,

Each stone, each clod, each seed, each tree, each flower,
Each running stream, fish, bird, and clime, all! all!
I see, I feel the rapture of this light.
I've wept, and prayed, and suffered much,
But this o'erjoys, and makes me rich indeed.
Oh, Rome! I'll pray for thee. Henceforth I'll labor
The folds of darkness hanging dense around
The Vatican to tear away. Helpme
Ye angels! Through churches, monasteries, the light
Swift winged shall go.

    Bran. and Fitz H.   Amen! Amen!
Be light 'mong Afric's sunny heart-warm children,
Oh shine on Asia's millions, Sun Divine!
Oh angels bright disperse the clouds, and bathe
The world in glory.

    Bran. points.) See what moves this way.

(*Enter spirit of Protestant divine.*)

  Spirit. The churches all are drifting, all are drifting.
Dead is the heart of our theology.
An angry Father slaying his only Son
To satsify his wrath, scarce credence finds.
They toss about decrees, foreordination, and all such
As children do soap-bubbles for their pastime.
The press is now the teacher, not the pulpit.
Alas! alas! oh! oh!! oh! oh—h—h! alas!   [*Exit.*

(*Enter spirit of priest holding a cross.*)

  Spirit. The spring floods rise The winter's ice is
    broken.
The church is drifting, drifting. Splendid rites
No more avail. No more avails us now
The ministerial lineage. Wheels! oh wheels
Of progress stop! Where, oh where will you bear us?
And must we change? The young, the old say "yes."
Alas! alas! oh! oh!! oh! oh—h—h! alas!   [*Exit*

*Two girls, dressed one in blue, the other in red, holding
one a banner with the word "Science," the other a
banner with the words "Progress of the Age," appear
holding by the hand a young lady dressed as a bride
in white.*

  Science. My glory is to sit beneath thy feet and learn.

Progress of the Age. To herald thy advancing march,
my duty.

Bride. To-day who will decide what is the truth?
We need a revelation which displays
The light without a shadow of the false.
Such now we have. Through it we causes see.
Through it up to the triune heavens we go;
Through it we see the angels, and their lives behold.
Their bosom joys, their past and future histories,
And thence th' unfoldings of the Infinite.

(A chant by the three

And he that sat upon the throne said "behold I make
all things new." [*Exeunt.*

Fitz H. Strange sights, strange sounds, that truth
will reign is sure.

Bran. The Old now vanishes away. The New
Speeds on its heaven appointed glorious course.
[*Church bell rings.*

Antonicelli. There sounds the solemn vesper bell. Its
summons
I must attend.

Bran. That bell's sweet silvery tones
Now thrills within the spirit harp, and all
My soul does burn to hear the vesper song.

Fitz Hugh. And mine is kindled too.

Antonicelli. Come, let's away. [*Exeunt.*
(W.

SCENE 2. *Colorado. A street in Denver.*

Enter TIM RILEY *and* PAT SYMES.

Tim R. Pat, do you know Conwell, who owns the
rich mine, Mexican Cacique?

Symes. Yes. Tim, I remimber him.

Tim R. He is now in Spain, but will soon return and
settle at Manitou where he will breathe the sweet air of
the Garden of the Gods, and drink the nectar that bubbles up from the hearts of the rocks.

Symes. Good health to him, and a safe journey to his
own country, and may he bring a wife back with him.
Do ye mind.

Tim R. I think he will. Not a black eyed Señorita,

but a true American lady. Ah, Pat, when a man has
the whole world to choose from, he'll take a woman
born under the star spangled banner every time.

Symes. That's so, Tim. I mane to do that myself.
Do ye mind.

Tim R. Good day, Pat, and may you be married
within the year.   [*Exit.*

Symes. I say amin to that, for do ye mind, I need
some one to take care of me.

Enter stranger from the East.

Stranger. Fine day, sir. I'm picking up information
about mining and other things. Can you tell me what
a flume is?

Symes. Is it a flume you want to know? A flume is
this. Boards and beams all standing up just like the
Giant's Causeway, with water pouring through it just
like the fallen angels running from Gabriel's trumpet,
and tearing the earth up and carrying along big bowl-
ders like a bushel of peas swept down a mill stream.
That's a flume. Do ye mind.

Stranger. Will a flume wash down the Black Hills?

Symes Is it the Black Hills? Do ye mind. Black
is the color of disappintment and death. Do ye mane
the hills where the naygurs live? The flume will carry
them off like so many jumping-jacks!

Stranger. Ha! ha! ha! The Black Hills I mean are
the hills where the miners wash out free gold.

Symes. Just so. I have ye there, do ye mind. The
hills in Californy are red like Cleopatra's hair. The
flume runs them off just like hot water all foaming from a
brewery. And the Black Hills will run down like Jim
Jones' lamp black all floating on the water. Do ye mind.

Stranger. But you will lose the gold.

Symes. Lose the gold! lose the gold! Why, do ye
mind, we catch that in the riggular way.

Stranger. How is that?

Symes. How's that? Why we introduce the quick-
silver, and that draws the gold like the North Pole the
needle, or like Mike Flynn's crooked whisky draws the
min afflicted with the epizooty. Do ye mind.

Stranger. Ha! ha! ha! I see sir. I presume you're
a miner.

Symes. Do ye mind. That's the trade of Emperors and Kings, and I'm a fellow craft.

Stranger. You have noble company. Have you any silver mines?

Symes. Is it silver mines? Have I any silver mines? I have as many silver mines as would take a crow a month of weeks to fly over, as much silver as would make Astors and Rothschilds of a million people. Do ye mind. And all my children will have silver spoons in their mouths. Do ye mind.

Stranger. Ha! ha! ha! Success to you, sir.

Symes. As sure as the American eagle keeps his wings spread out, there comes the church collector. For do ye mind, I haven't a cint to my name. There are holes in my pocket. I must be gone. Hold! he has turned the corner. That relieves me. Do ye mind.

Enter 'LIGE, the Denver prophet, ringing bell, with strip of muslin on back and on breast, with the words "Denver Stock Board, Twelve M."

'Lige. Now's de time to toss over de greenbacks and de silver dollars and de gold eagles. De stock shares be active as horse tails in fly time. Dey gwine up like a sky rocket. Now's de time. Procrastination is de tief of big fortunes. Let out de main sail, shake out de top gallant, run up de jib. De breezes in stocks blow stiff to-day. Now's de time. East Roe, Cash, Hercules, Victoria, and all de Pacific stocks.

Stranger. What is that Stock Board?

'Lige. Stock is de cattle. Stock board is de board for de cattle to go up on to de cars and to go down from de cars. De cars carry de stock. Dey go up bulls and come down b'ars.

Stranger. Ha! ha! ha! Great people out here. Facts are given with wonderful clearness and precision.

[*'Lige exit ringing, etc.*

Stranger. Perhaps you can tell me.

Symes. The stock board is the place where fortunes are made by rise in real estate, so it is. Do ye mind. You buy a share of mining ground, and all the gold under it, as yellow as the yelk of an egg, and rich as the ceiling of Solomon's temple. As soon as the gold comes

4

out your fortune's made. That's legitimate real estate business. Do ye mind.

Stranger. Joking aside, sir, what you now tell me is worth a whole year's series of magazine articles on the subject.

Symes. Do ye mind. There are two parts to me, the dispensable and the indispensable. With the dispensable I played foot-ball with you; with the indispensable I spake to the question.

Stranger. A little more of the indispensable, then.

Symes. Did you ever polish your heel on the curb of St. Bridget's well? Did you ever drink a cup of poteen to open your eyes Hallowmas night?

Stranger. No.

Symes. I thought so.

Stranger. Well, sir, does the Stock Board grow?

Symes. Did you ever see a young whale grow? You'll soon have to understand the harpoons, and the ropes, and the boats. Do ye mind. Does it grow? It will be the Be-he-moth of the nation. The big Comstock lode is only the jugular vein, but the heart is in Colorado, do ye mind. Here will be the Mammoth Stock Board. As it pulsates, so will the big money centres move.

Stranger. Bravo! sir. You think it useful, then?

Symes. Useful! Why, it's the fire that makes the stame that moves the whole machinery. It sells the stock and that opens the mines and develops them. It draws in the needful capital just like an alligator closing his jaws on a legion of flies settled in his mouth. Do ye mind.

Stranger. Good again, sir.

Symes. I must go or eat a cold dinner. Good day, sir.

Stranger. Good day, sir.

> [*Exeunt* STRANGER *and* SYMES.

SCENE 3. *Spain. Madrid. Parlor in* DON SEBASTIANO'S *palace.*

DON SEBASTIANO *and* DON GOMEZ *playing at cards.*

Don Seb. Miss Chadwell's lover, Brantley, so I hear,
To Spain's bright capital soon wends his way.

Don G. Unless delays unlooked for step between
Him and his coming.

> [DON SEBASTIANO *rises, then* DON GOMEZ.

Don Seb. Hem! suppose, Don Gomez,
We form a plot to extricate Miss Chadwell,
Cheat vigilance, and force dark chance to aid
Her lover. This will drive away ennui.

Don G. Agreed! the plot.

Don Seb. That old duenna aunt
Deals with her lovely niece most barbarously.
'Tis plain she wants to wed her to a noble.
The suitor's role I'll act, and we together
Well schooled in love's devices, soon will bring
The niece and Brantley face to face.

Don G. I fear it will be difficult
To win this Brantley to our artful plans.
He shrinks from aught unseemly, and prefers
All pain to suffer than give others pain.

Don Seb. We'll draw his friend, whose swollen purse o'erflows
With ducats, into the secrets of our strategy.
Persuasion will shake off the lover's scruples.
My part, then, is to play the love-sick suitor;
The niece I'll take to garden, or cathedral;
And you the aunt to museum, or palace.
Thus Brantley meets his lady and myself;
The work of chance will seem this sudden meeting;
A strauger's guise will mask my recognition;
I'll feign a little jealousy and hauteur;
But yet on some well timed pretence I'll ope
The way for Brantley to declare his love.
Her hand engaged, the rest in time will follow.
The aunt's roused wrath we will appease, and heal
Her wounded pride.

Don G. The scheme is good and simple.
To take fresh counsel let us daily meet.

Don Seb. This very hour the aunt, and niece, to see
My grounds, conservatories, picture halls,
And all my curiosities, are coming.

Don G. This suits our plan—

[*Enter* MRS. PERCY *and* MISS CHADWELL.

Don Seb. and Don G. Good day, ladies.

Don Seb. You're punctual, Señora, to the moment.

Mrs. Percy. We leave not till the round of sights we
close.

Th' Alhambra charmed my niece's tongue and fancy,
The Hall of Lions, and the Garden, too,
They gave her such delight. 'Tis wondrous pity
The Moors could not return, and occupy
That sunny land. 'Tis pity they were banished.

Don G. The Spaniards love to boast the noble relics
Of art, and wealth, and rare refinement found
In Andalusia's kingly palaces.
But in Madrid are sights of wonder, too ;
And beyond her walls are scenic vistas grand,
And ruins old of by gone chivalry.
As escort to those haunts, and memories,
That thrill, and pulse the proud Castilian's heart,
Señora Percy will command my service.

Don Seb. My service begs acceptance too, Miss
  Chadwell.

Mrs. Percy. You'll rob me of my niece's company.

Don Seb. We you would please, Señora, but yet hope
You'll not forego this timely proffered escort.

Mrs. Percy. Well, be it so.

Don G. (*Offers his arm.*) Señora, let us lead
The way into the garden.

Don Seb. (*Offers his arm to Miss C.*) We will follow.
                                      [*Exeunt.*

(*Ring Drop.*)

ACT IV.

SCENE 1. *Same as Scene 3, Act 3.*

DON SEBASTIANO *seated at table writing, rises holding
  letters.*

Don Seb. One single day has thrown a spell around
  me.
Sincerity has fled into her castle.
No arts will draw her thence. Sebastiano,
Thou wert sincere when Gomez talked with thee.
But now my mind is changed. A power above me
Whispers thus, "win her for yourself. Be this the bent,
The purpose, high ambition of your being."
It must be so. There's none in all the world

Like her. She's peerless, fit to sit the queen
Of this proud monarchy. Such thoughts, such language,
Such purity, such character, such grace ;
In charms a Venus. And who is this Brantley ?
A simple, thoughtful priest, a visionary too,
I'm told. Why help him, and thus mar myself ?
No! no! To act the double part is now
Expedient. Gomez will advise and counsel,
Yet all his schemes I'll balk, and baffle.
The surest way to rid me of all trouble,
Is to get Brantley home. These forged letters
Will hurry him across the billowy ocean.
I'll use all arts to inflame the aunt against him.
I'll use money, brains, experience to gain
My suit. It will be strange if I cannot
Outwit them all. Ho! Carlos! Carlos!
   (*enter* CARLOS.)   Here!
These letters take to Philip Juan Hernandez.
This card directs. Be quick, and bring his answer.
                       [*Exit* CARLOS.
Thus swift my purpose flies to its fulfilment.

      Enter MAUD, *the Gypsy Queen.*

Ah, Maud! your feet have lent obedient speed.
Encamp to-morrow early near San Pedro,
The church where holy fountains pour their streams.
A sweet enchanting lady will come with me,
And meet you there. Our fates you will divine.
Warn her against a priest, a prying thoughtful priest,
Who peers into the spirit world, and tells
Of what the angels do. Press her to look
On me with favor. Your guerdon will be large.
   Maud. To-morrow morn your wishes I'll obey.
                     [*Exit* MAUD.
     Enter HERNANDEZ. *Hands letter to* DON SEB.
Hernandez, thanks! How all things work together.
   Hernan. As you this morn directed me, I gave a roll
Of ducats to the postal clerk, who gave
To me this letter.
   Don Seb.   Met you not my page ?
   Hernan. No Señor.
   Don Seb.   He's gone with letters to your home—
Call in an hour.   [*Exit* HERNAN.

Don Seb. *opens letter and reads:*
"My Friend Conwell—
.   I must relinquish the thought of visiting
Madrid at present. The visit would afford me much
pleasure, if it did not induce Mrs. Percy to shorten her
stay in that lovely city. I will therefore postpone my
visit.   Yours ever,
                              Charles Brantley."
Good! good! this harmonizes with my plans.
This new priest freshly come, Antonicelli,
They much esteem, and urge his frequent visits.
He's good and pious, and serves my turns
Without his knowing it. His burning zeal
And eloquence will soon convert the aunt
And niece to our religion. Then my love
Will move her pity, and at length prevail.
                  Enter Don Gomez.
    Don Seb. Don Gomez, I declare. What plans to-day?
    Don Gom. The aunt with much reluctance gave
        consent
To view with me the moss-grown vine-clad ruins
Beyond the church San Pedro.
    Don Seb.   That's well, Don Gomez.
Do you attend the royal ball to-night?
    Don G. My ear will bend to other music.
    Don Seb.   Ah! the voice
Of one you love. Success to you, my friend.
    Don G. Adios. Beso los manos.   [*Exit* Don G.
    Don Seb. (*Puts letter on table.*)   Carlos! Carlos!
        (*Rings a bell.*) ·*Enter* Joanna.
    Don Seb. Has Carlos not returned?
    Joanna.   Not as yet, Señor.
    Don Seb. If one Hernandez comes, tell him to stay
Till I return.
    ·*Joanna.* Yes, Señor.   [*Exit* Don Seb.
    Joanna. Dear me, I must put this room in order.
What is brewing, I wonder? So many people coming
and going. Something ails Señor. How excited he
looks. I can see bird's eggs when the nest is in the
grass. When the cream is on the cat's whiskers, I guess
she has visited the milk pan. When the bird flutters
without power to fly, I guess a charmer is near. All
things have their signs. Señor's face is flushed, his

blood leaps wildly, like that of a man in a fever. Sure sign that the poison of cupid's arrow rankles. Didn't I watch him as he walked and talked with that beautiful lady? I felt sure he was falling in love. What's this? A letter to Mr. J. Conwell. Why that's Alfonso's Señor. I must read this. (*Reads.*) I wonder if Alfonso brought this from Señor Conwell? Why didn't he come into the servant's hall to see me? I must scold him for this. (*Hears footsteps, puts down letter. Enter* CARLOS.) Come, Carlos, help me. Will Señor be gone long?

Carlos. No, he returns soon. Can you keep a secret, Joanna?

Joanna. Can the ocean hold fish? I'm no cackling hen. Anything about Alfonso?

Carlos. No. It's a big secret.

Joanna. Well, what is it?

Carlos. Antonia, Mrs. Percy's page, got a purse of gold to say "not at home" to Miss Russell and Miss Travers.

Joanna. Who gave it to him?

Carlos. I don't know, but I can guess.

Joanna. So can I guess. I must run.

[*Exit* JOANNA.

(w)   *Bell rings. Exit* CARLOS.

SCENE 2. *Street in Madrid. House with open window.*

Enter two SERVANTS.

1st Serv. I am miserable. My poor heart weighs me down.

2d Serv. Are you importing a lead cargo?

1st Serv. I have lost my heart.

2d Serv. Lost all your ballast and weighed down?

1st Serv. Yes, weighed down, gravitated down like a collapsed balloon.

2d Serv. Ha! ha! ha! Cupid's lance didn't draw much blood till now.

1st Serv. You say the truth. My pulse will hardly beat 30 to the minute. The fact is, my heart is water-logged. If things don't change I'll be foundered.

2d Serv. You are in a pitiable plight. Who is the fair Dulcinea?

1st Serv. Joanna.

2d Serv. Joanna! Why that's Alfonso's sweetheart.

Enter from R. *scissors grinder. Enter from* L. *glazier.*

Scis. G. Scissors to grind?

Glaz. Glass to put in?

1st Serv. to Scis. G. I am in luck. You are the very man I want. Call at Mrs. Percy's at 2 o'clock.

Scis. G. I'll be even with the shadow, on the sun dial.

[*Exit* 1st SERVANT.

2d Serv. to Glazier. You are come in sight just in time. Call at Don Sebastiano's at 2 o'clock.

Glaz. I'll be as punctual as the sun that moves the shadow.   [*Exit* 2d SERVANT.

Scissors grinder and glazier put down their packs.

Glaz. Do you want a pair of glass eyes?

Scis. G. Lay your tongue on my grindstone and I'll give it a new edge.

Glaz. Did you ever sharpen a wasp's sting? On your grindstone, I think, my tongue will soon cease to be a Damascus blade.

Scis. G. Without me, where would be the swords that smite down the king's enemies?

Glaz. Without me, the palaces of kings and queens would be dark and cheerless.

(*Woman appears at window.*)

Scis. G. Scissors to grind?

Glaz. Glass to put in?

Woman. Can you sharpen the shears of fate? And can you make the wheel of fortune transparent with glass?

Scis. G. I'll try my skill.

Glaz. And I'll try mine.

Woman. Then shoulder your packs and call on Madame Destiny, Scissors to grind? Glass to put in?

They shoulder their packs and stand under the window and bawl out,

Madame Destiny, scissors to grind?

Madame Destiny, glass to put in.

Woman. Away, you varlets!

Scis. G. Madame Destiny, scissors to grind?

Woman Away, I say; be gone!

Glaz. Madame Destiny, glass to put in?

Woman. Stop that bawling under my window!

Scis. G. Madame Destiny, scissors to grind?

Glaz. Madame Destiny, glass to put in?

Woman. Go away! what will people say?

Scis. G. Madame Destiny, scissors to grind?

Glaz. Madame Destiny, glass to put in?

Woman. (*Screams.*) Help! go away, I tell you!

Man appears at window.) [*Crowd gathers, laughs*

Woman. There they are, the horrid things.

Scis. G. Madame Destiny, scissors to grind?

Glaz. Madame Destiny, glass to put in?

　　　　　　　　　　[*Man rushes out of door.*

Man. 　　　　　　Be gone, you scoundrels!

Scis. G. Madame Destiny, scissors to grind?

Glaz. Madame Destiny, glass to put in?

　　Enter police, catches irate man.)

Police. What is all this uproar about?

Man. These fellows are insulting my wife.

　　　　　　　　　　　[*Crowd laugh.*

Scis G. Madame Destiny, scissors to grind?

Glaz. Madame Destiny, glass to put in?

Woman rushes out and falls on neck of her husband.

Woman. Don't take him. Don't take him.

Scis. G. Madame Destiny, scissors to grind?

Glaz. Madame Destiny, glass to put in?

Police. Come along all of you; come Madame.

Scis. G Madame Destiny, scissors to grind?

Glaz. Madame Destiny, glass to put in?

Police. Be silent there. 　[*Crowd laughs*

w) 　　　　　　　　[*Exeunt all.*

SCENE 3. *Garden and fountain near San Pedro Church.*
Gipsy camp.
Enter DON GOMEZ *and* MRS. PERCY.

Mrs. Percy. The gipsies love to camp in sweet
romantic
Retired spots, where many flowers and fountains
Will cast a charm about their tented life.

Don Gom. Señora Percy, this is Maud, our gipsy
queen.
She knows my family and predicts its fortunes.
Please try her skill.
　　　　　5

Maud. (*Takes her left hand.*)
You have longevity outpictured here ;
Vast wealth ; your sister died some time ago ;
Her daughter is your chief and only care.
She loves a good pure minded man, a priest.
This used to grieve you much. The hour draws near
When grief will cease. I see a change in you ;
An unexpected meeting far away ;
Your niece's destiny will then be shaped.
 Don Gom. Now, Maud, try mine.
 Maud.   A fair and gentle hand
Is to be joined to yours in holy wedlock.
A land and water journey is before you ;
Great hills all seamed with gold and silver ores
You'll see. A happy future yours, Don Gomez.
 Don Gom. Thanks Maud (*Gives her gold.*) Adios.
       [*Exeunt* DON G. *and* MRS. P

 (MAUD *gives a low whistle ; two boys appear.*)
 Maud. Silverio, go see if Sebastiano's coming. Joachimo, see when Don Gomez passes out of sight. Hurry back both of you (*Exeunt boys*) I must tell the truth and not the truth to please Sebastiano. I will not tell him all I see. I want his well filled purse, and will so speak.   [*Enter* SILVERIO.
 Silv. I see the horses of Don Sebastiano coming fast.
         [*Enter* JOACHIMO.
 Joa Don Gomez has passed out of sight.
 Maud. My darlings, now retire. I see them coming.
 Enter DON SEBASTIANO *and* MISS CHADWELL.
 Don Seb. The race of gipsies dates far back ; they boast
Descent from Ishmael and are Bedouins
In nature. Old astrology is claimed
By them as all their people's heritage,
And palmistry which they with pride derive
From patriarchal days. The book of Job
Tells its antiquity. This is the queen.
Your name please deign to give.
 Maud   My name is Maud.
 Don Seb. This lady fair and I would try your skill.
 Maud. (*takes* MISS CHADWELL's *left hand.*)

Your stars are happy in their various aspects ;
Also the lines of destiny herein
Displayed Great riches you possess. A cross
In love is manifest. A priest appears
Who reads the stars and searches into things
Of hidden nature. Spirits he beholds
And angels, and reveals the future age.
His star looks east. In Rome he stays at present ;
Your signs diverge. Another comes in view ;
He draws your sign to his. He is a noble
Of great possessions, learned, wise, and generous.
His love is strong. To you he opens place
And power ; I see a crown advancing too ;
This is the way to highest fortune. Choose
This road ; so say the stars.

    Maud.   Now hold your hand.
The nation seeks your hand to guide her fates.
This lady's sign and yours have come together.
If they remain it shows a speedy marriage,
Great joy, great riches, and thick clustering honors.

    Don Seb. (*Gives purse to* MAUD.)
Thanks and adios, Maud. Now for the ruins
                  [*Exeunt* DON SEB *and* MISS C.
    Maud. This purse will make us merry, merry gipsies.
                 [MAUD *retires out of sight.*

(w)

        SCENE 4. *A street in Madrid.*

      Enter CONWELL *and* DON GOMEZ.

    Con. The fate foretelling art is sometimes useful.
You look annoyed, to-day ; perhaps recourse
To gipsey Maud will help you—
    Don Gom.   Solve the riddle.
    Con. What riddle? that Sebastiano ?
    Don Gom.   Yes.
I visit and consult with him. He seems
To yield consent to all my plans and yet—
    Con. Takes care to follow that which suits him best.
    Don Gom. Just so. You read him well. He wants
      to serve
Himself, not Brantley. What so keeps our friend ?
His stay makes me Sebastiano's dupe
Appear.

Con. Don Gomez, I do gossip hate;
But yet to-day I lent reluctant ear
To what my valet felt constrained to tell.
My valet's tattling lover who hears much
And sees more at Sebastiano's mansion,
Relates that she, a letter from my friend
Charles Brantley, saw upon the parlor table
To my address. And also that the page
Antonio had gold received to say
To lady friends of ours, " Señora Percy
Is not at home."

Don Gom. If this be true, he is
A very monster. This news sets my blood
On fire.

Con. Restrain yourself, my friend. You asked
Why Brantley was delayed? Perhaps his letters
Have intercepted been.

Don Gom. I see it now.
Sebastiano thought our wrath to kindle
Against the aunt and niece, and break beyond
Repair the sacred vase that held our friendship.
Just what he wants. He thus can hunt with horse
And hounds the forest through and no one say
Him nay.

Con. The game he plays is bold and earnest.
That move was false It turns the game against him.
To match his skill, two wills now bend their thoughts.
Intrigue I do not like. But this is for
My friend; it is for her he loves: it is
Foul wrong to check and smother villainy.
You know Antonicelli?

Don Gom. Yes, quite well.

Con. He's one of Brantley's warmest friends

Don Gom. A strong
Ally within the citadel.

Con. Acquaint
Him with the situation and his help
Secure.

Don Gom. I will, this very hour.

Con. Meet me
At noon. Be cool and cautious *Exeunt.*
w

SCENE 5. *Madrid. Room in* MRS. PERCY'S *house*

Enter MRS. PERCY.

Mrs. Percy. Antonicelli, holy pious father,
By whom the day spring streaming from the skies
Dispels the mists and shadows of my soul,
Thy words have changed me   Now the world's
      ambitions
Disturb no more more my rest. The end of life
Is not position, fortune, fleeting pleasure ;
But 'tis to attain God's image in the soul.
I see i now. I cannot shut it out.
Oh time! my misspent time! my earthly days
Are nearly numbered. A life of uses
Transforms the soul. Can I redeem the past?
I deem'd he was a fool. Antonicelli
Thinks him a chosen witness to the truth.
I think so, too   Soon to Madrid he comes ;
I then will send for him. Be gone, my pride!
I then *will* send for him. I hated him :
I hated the very name ; but now my heart
Will yearn to see him, and his name's as music
Of angel voice and harp. Yes Brantley, Brantley
Despised once but now esteemed friend.
The rich, the great admire my noble niece.
She none accepts. She still for Brantley lives.
Must I reverse my oft declared purpose?
Down! down! My tempter down! I *will* reverse it

Enter MISS CHADWELL.

Miss Chadwell. Antonicelli has just gone. Through
   him
There speeds some news that near concerns us.
Against señora Percy and her niece
Two Spanish Dons conspired—

Mrs. Percy.   Who are the Doas?
Miss Chadwell. They are Sebastiano and Don Gomez.
Mrs. Percy And what did they conspire?
Miss Chadwell.   To render null
Your wary vigilance, defeat your will,
And then appease your anger.

Mrs. Percy.   Ha! I see
Their plans.

Miss Chadwell. Not all, dear aunt. Sebastiano
Deceived Don Gomez.

Mrs. Percy. He to us appeared
The serious lover.

Miss Chadwell. Yes, but double tongued.
How did he speak to you of Brantley, aunt?

Mrs. Percy. He spoke to me of him with pious pity
As one deluded ; as unfit for aught
But dreamy reveries suited to a cloister.

Miss Chadwell. To me he spoke of him admiringly,
As wise and good. His words conveyed the thought
That he was Brantley's sworn and dearest friend.

Mrs. Percy. I see it all.

Miss Chadwell Not all, dear aunt. Your page
Antonio admittance to deny
To both our dear most prized lady friends
Was bribed.

Mrs. Percy. This quite amazes me.

Miss Chadwell. A letter
To Conwell sent from Rome has been purloined.
And now, dear aunt, just hold your breath awhile ;
Charles Brantley Rome has left e're now to cross
The broad Atlantic.

Mrs. Percy. Now I see it all.
Who would believe that one so noble could
Thus stoop so low. Charles Brantley goes—we follow.
Another morn shall see us on our way
To Paris. I must haste to give my orders. [*Exit.*

Miss Chadwell. It seems unkind in me, against
      Sebastiano
To turn my aunt, to change her good opinion
And nip the tender blooming buds of friendship.
But all duplicity I hate. His purpose
Guaged by the world, is highly flattering.
But though crowned heads should seek my hand and
      stoop
To meanness, I would scorn their thrones and sceptres.
The soul that wills to lose all hopes, all joys ;
That wills to pass a life of weariness
And pain, a desolated heart to bear
In uncomplaining meekness, rather than
Resort to stratagem, or plant a crown

Of thorns upon another's brow, that soul
I honor, although artisan or peasant,
Though walking on earth's lowest social round,
But I must go and hurry preparations.   [*Exit.*
  (w)

SCENE 6. *Madrid. Plain room in* SEBASTIANO'S *palace.*

Enter SEBASTIANO

Don Seb.   Beyond my grasp the prize is gone, I fear.
What sudden impulse hurried them away?
Oh that I were a monarch absolute!
Their course I would arrest within the hour.
Yes, down in dungeon deep that wily aunt
I'd thrust. Oh! how reproachfully she looks!
Right here she stands and seems to read my thoughts.
Bright angel, stay! oh stay! yes stay! Miss Chadwell!
The vision's gone. Who can explain this mystery?
Oh! oh! this pain! this agony! my heart!
My heart be still! Why did I love her so?
                    (*Enter* CARLOS.)
Don Seb.   What's that?
Carlos.   A letter, Señor.
Don Seb.   Hand it here
  (*Reads.*)   [*Exit* CARLOS.
"To Don Sebastiano."
It is from her; I almost fear to read
Its contents.
  (*Opens and reads.*)   I write this at the sea coast. My
aunt desires me to thank you for all your kind attentions,
but frankly adds that she hopes you never will resort to
dishonorable means to attain an honorable purpose, and
beg me to say for her, adios, and may heaven change
your heart and bless your life. And I, too, say adios
                    MARY CHADWELL.
          (*Crushing the letter in his hand.*)
Sebastiano's baffled, yes baffled. All vain
My hopes to win her now. That gipsy Maud
Foretold—that's nonsense—of our signs foretold,
If they together stood, our marriage then
Soon would ensue. She then this parting saw.
Just now it looks that Brantley yet will meet her.

Sebastiano's baffled, yes baffled. Madrid
Will hum with rumors now. "She's jilted him"
Will run from mouth to mouth. Consigned to flames
   (*Burns the letter at a candle.*)
This letter perishes. Now, then, I'll be
Myself again. Oh, Señorita Chadwell!
Oh, Maria! Maria!
   Enter ANTONICELLI.
Antonicelli, you are come too late.
The ship that carries them has sailed e're this
I sent to talk with you about my future,
Bright spangled o'er with beaming hopes, just like
A studded sky without a cloud at midnight.
The vision's fled, Antonicelli; now
A blank, a painful void remains. Come out
With me and let us talk together; I
Am glad you're come.   [*Exeunt*
 (W)

  SCENE 7.—*Garden in Stockholm -Snowing.*

   Enter BRANTLEY.

 Bran. Four changeful weeks with shortening days
  I've rambled
To see old Sweden's features, and now haste
To escape stern Winter who, with sudden leap,
Has passed the barriers of the freezing zone
And here reigns drearily; his chariot speeding
Of driving storm and sleet, all nature drowsing
To sleep beneath his snowy coverlets,
And deep clear heaven reflecting lakes close sealing
With thick pellucid ice. The sheltering eaves
The twittering birds in flocks receive. Around
The burdened trees surge heavily and sigh
Before the howling blast. The mammoth bears
Now hybernate. In rooty chambers lies
Locked up the Summer's glory to live anew
In leaf and bud and fruit, when earth
Has rolled again through half her orbit.
Now Stockholm veiled in fast falling flakes
Will soon recede to my admiring gaze.
But Sweden's water-falls of silver-curling spray

Sometimes descending quick in pure white sheets
Of foaming airiness, or fluttering
Into lace-woven curtain draperies,
In memory's sunniest halls will always gleam.
I must find Koogland, greet and bid adieu
In the same breath.   [*Exit.*

  (W.)

SCENE 8.—*Stockholm. Parlor in* KOOGLAND'S *house.*

Enter KOOGLAND.

Koog. I love my native land, her skies her hills
And lakes, those lakes so clear, sharp pointed rocks
Far down beneath appear to rise and touch
The gliding boat, her fame, her wisdom, courage.
Forget thee, No, my country, no! Around
Thee, Stockholm too, cling the tendrils of my soul ;
Thou Northern Venice, now in ice and snow
Enshrouded, now in verdure, music, beauty
Anew revealed with magic suddenness ;
Thy palace crowned social terraced homes,
The flashing Mœlar's thousand isles beholding ;
All this I leave through potency of love
By secret hope impelled to see what fate
Awaits a second effort.

Enter SERVANT.—SERVANT *gives* card.—KOOGLAND
reads.

                 Rev. Charles Brantley.
Our welcome give.   [*Exit servant.*
               This is a vast surprise.
I'll haste to greet him.

Enter BRANTLEY.

Koog.   Brantley, welcome! welcome!
This meeting quite surpasses my conception.
  Bran. Some seek the birth place of the English bard
And some the tomb-stone of the Roman poet,
But I the land of the great Sage, the pride
Of Sweden.
  Koog.   So he's not unknown to you?
  Bran. He's so well known to me, that all the world
               6

His heavenly revelations soon may learn,
Is now my constant prayer.
    Koog.   Stay you some time
In Stockholm?
    Bran.   No, friend Koogland, haste now calls me
To Hamburg first and thence America
    Koog. Within this very hour I bid farewell
To home and country on my route to Hamburg.
    Bran. Give me your hand. We'll meet at noon
    Koog.   But stay!
My father will rejoice to see you.
    Bran.   No.
Time forbids. Adieu.   [*Exit Brantley.*

Enter KOOGLAND's *Father*

    K. Father. This form once upright chilling age sore
    presses
With his increasing weight. My son, my Charles,
You will not go and leave your dear old father?
    Koog. Dear father, here my days are all misspent;
My life is purposeless; I need the change;
My poor sad heart is far across the sea,
Dear father.
    K. Father.   My dear son, cannot that wound
Be healed?
    Koog.   No, no, it's vain to try. I'll soon
Return—

Enter SERVANT.

    Serv.   The sleigh's prepared and waiting stands.
                      [*Exit servant.*

KOOGLAND *and Father embrace.*

My son! what will your dear old father do
While you are gone? Oh, Charles! my son! my son!
Farewell! farewell!
  (*Ring Slow Drop.*)

ACT V.

SCENE 1. *Louisiana.—Negro cabin at Mrs.* PERCY'S *home.- Negroes, men and women.—Old Jo and granny and young Jo. — Table set out for a feast.*

Old Gran. Ole missis and young missis look so well.
[*Young Jo jumps round and shouts.*

Young Jo. Oh! I'se so glad! Missis come home.
[*Sings.*

Hear de kullered angels holler ;
"Is you ready for de skies?"
Hear de kullered angels holler ;
"Wake up darkies, win de prize."

CHORUS.
Singing, dancing, singing, dancing,
Sing and dance, oh sing and dance.

Old Gran. Stop chile! stop! you won't lef ole folkes talk. [*Boy sings.*

Hear de kullerd angels holler ;
"Open wide de heabenly gate ;"
Hear de kullered angels holler ;
"Walk in darkies, 'fore's too late."

CHORUS.
Singing &c.

Old Jo. What ails de boy? He be crazy.
[*Boy shouts.*

Hear de kullerd angels holler ;

Old Jo. Yes boy, yes boy, we hear 'em. Play de banjo dare. [*All sing.*

TUNE, *Angel Boatman.*

1. Waken in de midnight lonely,
   All we darkies thought we feel,
Dat de white folks gone, and only
   Shaddurs true de cabin steal.

CHORUS.

Oh dese hearts day trob and quibber
  Wid de dulcet toues of peace ;
Glory for de blessed gibber,
  Now and nebber, nebber cease

2. Each returnin' night de shaddurs,
  Like some spectres, peered to rise.
And we darkies feered day hab us,
  'Fore we'd see our missis eyes.   [*Chorus.*

3. We be happy, happy people,
  Cause de white folkes hab come home :
And we'll holler from de steeple,
  Day's from home no more to roam. [*Chorus.*

Old Jo. Dis animates us. (*Seizes old Granny, each takes a partner.*) Come all. Play de banjo dare.
[*All dance, and boy sings.*
"Hear de kullered angels holler."

Enter Mrs. PERCY *and Miss* CHADWELL.

Old Gran. Oh, Missis, we's so glad. Dat boy gone distracted wid joy, cause Missis come home. Go way chile ! Stop dat noise !

Miss C. Jo! Jo! Jo!

Young Jo. Yes, Missis.

Miss C. Jo, call Jim, be quick.   [*Exit Young Jo.*

Mrs. Percy. I hope you will all have a good time. Jo will bring some fruit.

Old Jo & Gran. Thank you Missis.
[*Exeunt Mrs. P. and Miss C.*

Old Jo. Come, sit down granny, come sit down all. (*Old Jo says grace.*) May de blessins of hebben rain down on ole missis and young missis ; may de skies of der life shine like de mornin's sun ; and all de corncribs break wid de corn ; and de tables tremble wid de fowles of de air and beasts of de field, for ebber and ebber. Amen.

Enter Jo *and* JIM *with fruit.— Young Jo sings as they enter.*

"Hear de kullered angels holler, &c."

Old Gran. I'se hab to choke de bref out of dat chile.

Old Jo. No use granny, no use, we must get up and dance way de joy 'fore we can eat. (*Old Jo and all ri's* Put back de table. Clar de way. Get de banjo dare. [*All dance.—Jo and Jim join hands and dance wildly, singing, "Hear de kullered &c."—Granny stops dancing with Jo then all stop.*

Gran. I hab an interestin' and 'portant circumstance to tell.

Old Jo. Well, granny, what's de circumstance?

Gran. We's all happy Jo, and you's happy.

Old Jo. Yes, dat's so, granny.

Gran. Missis come home and we's glad.

Old Jo. Yes, granny, and de circumstance.

Gran. You'll 'scuse me Jo, but 'tis somethin' 'portant and 'tickler.

Old Jo. Well, granny.

Gran. I want you to 'low me somethin'.

Old Jo. What's dat granny? You shall hab it on dis 'spicious occasion, to de half of my kingdom.

Gran. Well, I speck I hab to tell.

Old Jo. Yes, granny, do tell.

Gran. I want you—to—'low me—to—voto.

[*Old Jo throws arms out and starts back amazed*

Gran. Well, I declar Jo, you look like cannon ball hit you durin' de war.

Old Jo. Yes, granny, I'm tunder struck. Woman vote? My ole granny vote? Whar will be my manhood then?

Gran. Dear Jo, dear Jo, just say yes—you promus me de half of your kingdom, you won't break de promus, Jo?

Old Jo. Well, granny, to-morrow I'se give my answer. Dat's 'portant sure enough. Play de banjo dare.

[*All dance.*

Enter Miss CHADWELL.

Miss C. Come out and see the fireworks and afterward go on with the dance.

[*Exit Miss C. All follow, young Jo in rear.*

Young Jo. Hurrah! blue lights and sky-rockets! Sing and dance, oh, sing and dance.

(w.)

SCENE 2. – *Same as scene 2, Act 1st.*

Enter TIM. RILEY *and* PAT SYMES *with wheelbarrow full of flower-pots.*

Symes. Well, Tim, life's all a drame. The flowers here nod to us as old acquaintance. I'm certain they will never feel the knife any more to make a bouquet for the bishop. Do ye mind.

Tim. His wine has turned sour. We see this in the figures made by the shifting of the house kaleido-cope. His chances are all run out like the sands of the old retired doctor.

Symes. Experience has made me a wiser man too, Tim. Do ye mind. I was once as rich as Mrs. Percy, if I had only succeeded in getting it out of the ground. But some cruel necromancer put a spell on it (perhaps the old bishop's prayers did it) and there it sticks fast in the hard rocks to this day. Do ye mind.

Tim. It is true, Pat. There is a secret power around us that gives or withholds wealth. We may find rich mines, unless this secret power helps us, vain our hopes to realize. It's so in love, in business, and all life affairs. I'm content to stay here and nurse the flowers. This is happiness after all, Pat.

Symes. You reason like a solon, Tim. Do ye mind. What's the use in all the crazy efforts to be rich? A rich mine collects a crowd of sharp lawyers and unprincipled villains, like buzzards to a carcass, each anxious to gorge himself. Do ye mind. I feel satisfied to stay as I am and smoke the pipe of contentment. I have done with fortune hunting, Tim. Do ye mind.

[*Horn is blown.*

Tim. There's the dinner horn. Let us be going.

[*Exeunt.*

SCENE 3.—*Parlor at Mrs.* PERCY'S.—*Same as scene 1.*
Act 1

Enter Miss CHADWELL *and Miss* FLORENCE.

Miss C. The views we meet, in Alps or Appenines
Your mountain scenes excel. One view remains
Firm set in memory. Mount Blanc uplifts

Its snow-draped head with silent mystery crowned,
While all around is dark and stars yet hold
Their sway, to catch the ruby glow
Of morning's mystic baptism ; which dissolves
As down the mountain's side the nimble light,
With swift descending steps, compels the gloom
In hurried flight to cast away her robes
All wet with vapor, and then slanting through
The vales, each blade of grass, each leaf of shrub
And tree, with sparkling dew-drops glistens.

   Miss F. Your vivid picture of that shrouded peak
Dispels all hope to paint in verbal colors
Our grand, and varied Rocky Mountain scenery.
It asks your eye, your ear, and glowing tongue
To speak aright its praises.

   Miss C.   Hush ! Miss Florence.
Just tell about the park wherein you camped.

   Miss F. Sweet memories cling around that park.
Each morn, each eve, some leaf, some flower inserted
Into the wreath of free and joyous life
I there experienced.   The air so pure
The blood in jocund mazes danced
With the exhilaration.   To the eye
This park seems like a congeries of parks.
At pleasing intervals stand verdant knolls
Whose summits spacious shady groves adorn,
While streams, in which the speckled trout disport,
Wind round and round between the knolls.
The level spaces seemed so regular
As if Dame Nature had surveyor turned,
And had with measuring chain the lines adjusted.
High shelving mountains hem this park around ;
The highest and the farthest are snow-crowned ;
While those below in living green are mantled
Of forests dense, of hemlock, spruce and pine.
Beneath our feet a rich bloom carpet spreads ;
And up the mountain's side, up to the verge
Of snow perpetual do bud and bloom
The glowing flowers ; there bees in hiving sweets
Do ply their busy toil ; and humming birds
That poise above each opening bud, their wings
Almost invisible ; the ptarmigan

With arctic plumage, and gray feathered grouse,
The coney in his rocky home, the deer,
The antelope, the mountain sheep and lion,
A living museum. The day we passed
In gathering flowers and lichens, fishing, reading
Or followed what the changing fancy prompted.
At night, within our tent, we heard the distant
Snow-slide, or dismal cayote howl. Sometimes
Near by the Indians pitched their tents, but gave
No whoop, nor sound of terror. I must stop.
Words fail to tell its beauties or its pleasures.
  Miss C. That park you Estes call. How unromantic!
To Colorado I must surely go   [*Bell rings.*
This very year. Come, see our century plant;
I hear the signal bell.   [*Exeunt.*

Enter Mrs. PERCY.

                       Where have they gone?
How true those bible words, "that many to
And fro shall go and knowledge be increased."
This era is the cosmopolitan,
The time for demolition of all barriers,
That stand between true hearts like prison walls.
All nations yet will be like angel sisters.
And all earth's families triune be, as are
The heavens. Now into human units men
Disintegrate, to fuse again in new
And lasting combinations. Flags tri-colored,
White, red and blue, o'er all the race shall float,
Truth representing in its three degrees;
And then equality, fraternity
And liberty will sway the world.

Enter Miss C. and Miss F.

  Miss C.   Aunt Percy
You are a French Communist.
  Mrs. P.   No, my niece—
  Miss F. The Century plant is quite magnificent.
Its flower superb.
  Mrs. P.   Through our magnolia groves
We drive to-morrow. When out West we go

And visit sunny, balmy Colorado—

Miss C. Plains you may find a garden, forests where
No tree, nor shrub appeared, and smiling homes
Where heretofore a desert. For you know
What you so often say, "There's nothing now
So strange as not to happen, nor so good
That it cannot be true, nor yet so high
That it cannot be reached."

Enter Bishop OBERHEIM.

Bp. Ob. What rare Utopia holds your thoughts to-
day?

Mrs. P. One that the dignities to-day conceive not.

Bp. Ob. Is it a beauteous dream, some fairy vision?

Mrs. P. We all rejoice in new found liberty.
Unrestrained air, and unimprisoned light
Less free than we in all their movements are,
No longer bound by creedal chains and fetters
Those leaden weights, that dead souls sink, no more
To rise.

Bp. Ob. This is not liberty, but license
You, like uncaged birds, will fly from tree
To tree, till lost, and cold, and weak, away
From home and nourishment, you'll die.

Miss C. Say rather
We'll find a new bright home, where sweet affection
To all our wants will minister, and pour down
Upon us heaven's own sunshine, and so knit
Our hearts to it, that never more we'll wander.

Mrs. P. Say not we'll find ; we have already found
That home.

Miss C. And from this home, love buoyed, its neck
Unfreighted by dull rolls of faith, each soul
Will mount and wing its joyful way, and meet
A welcome in its Father's house of rest.

Bp. Ob. Have you forsaken Mother Church?

Mrs. P. No, Bishop,
We only left our step-mother.

Bp. Ob. You pierce
My heart, dear ladies, you pierce my heart.
I little thought, that when I waved adieu
And bid God-speed to all your journeyings

7

In distant lands, that such a change I'd witness.
I'll weep, dear ladies, and I'll pray for you—

    Mrs. P. Do you remember what led me to cross
The treacherous sea?

    Bp. Ob. (*Points to Miss Chadwell.*) To bring the col-
      or to this cheek once faded,
But now so blooming, and your family
To save from a debas —unpleasant union.

    Mrs. P. It's through your counsels that in quiet haven
I'm anchored now. It's now my hope to see
And welcome to my heart, him upon whose neck
You pressed your iron heel.

    Bp. Ob.   Can it be Brantley?
Is it through him you've gone astray? I weep
For you, dear ladies.

    Mrs. P.   Spare your tears. We weep
For those who bow the neck and bend the knee
To mitred supercilious ignorance.

    Bp. Ob. (*Hurries away confused.*) Adieu.

Enter Old Jo.

    Mrs. P. Well Jo, did the Bishop send you here?

    Old Jo. No missis, not quite dat. I'se called to see
you 'bout 'portant matter 'tween me and granny.

    Mrs. P. You haven't quarrelled, Jo?

    Old Jo. No missis, not quite dat. She asked me 'fore
all de cabin to 'low her to vote. (*All ladies laugh.*)

    Miss. C. I suppose you said yes, of course, Jo?

    Old Jo. No, missis. I felt it too 'portant and thought
I'd see missis fust and ask her 'pinion. In de fust place,
whar will be ole Jo if granny votes? Jo will be no whar.
In de secon place, granny will tink nuthin of ole Jo
den. In de lass place, de young folks will 'gard me
nuthin'. I'ms lamentable 'bout it missis. Now, granny 'spects me to say yes. I promus her de half of my
kingdom, missis (*Ladies laugh*), and she holds me to de
promus. Now, just come and tell her. It will spare
my manhood some—let down my feelin's gentle, like de
water in de canal when day open de locks for de boat to
pass true. Come missis, come all.

            [*All laughing, follow Jo. Exeunt.*
  (W.)

SCENE 4.— *Wood scene.*

Enter Old Jo with wheelbarrow and hoe.

Its uncommon warm in de fields. But I must hoe de sweet potatoe crap. I 'spect de night tieves will grabble dem up 'fore day ripe. Howsomebber, I'll try one more crap. De white folks talk 'bout gwine 'way agin. Trabbel, trabbel all de time.

Enter Young Jo singing.

"Hear de kullered angels holler;"

Old Jo. Dat boy will sing spite of himself. Spare de rod and spoil de chile. Guess I'll hab to spoil him den.

Young Jo. Old Jo, whar's you gwine?

Old Jo. Boy, be more 'spectful; call me grand father or uncle Jo; that comes from 'lowing granny to vote.

Young Jo. Whar's you gwine with dis wheelbarrow? Let me ride, old Jo. (*Jumps in barrow.*)

Old Jo. Yes, chile. Spare de rod.

Young Jo. Sing and dance, sing and dance, whoop! whoop! (*Old Jo wheels off.*)

SCENE 5.—*Mrs.* PERCY'S *house and grounds.*

Enter Old Jo.

Old Jo. What ails de folks, day hardly settled down 'fore day go agin, like de wild ducks, day come down to eat and talk a little, den spread der wings and fly away. What comes dar?

Old Gran. Don't you know me, Jo?

Old J. How could I tell till you peered from 'hind de bush?

Old G. Missis is going certain.

Old J. Day are crowds of people to de party in dare.

Old G. Dat Swede man been so 'tentive to Miss Florence is dare. Do you 'spose he'll trabbel arter her?

Old Jo. I 'spects he will, granny. He keeps wid her all de time. He rides wid her, goes to church wid her, he's ebber dar.

Old G. She 'longs to Culuradur. Whar's dat, Jo?

Old Jo. Its off dat way whar de sun sets.

Old G. How came you here, Jo?

Old Jo. How came you here, granny?

Old G. I went out to shake way de lonesome feelin's creepin' over me.

Old Jo. And I went out to be alone and let de tear drops fall. It's too bad, granny, too bad, dat day go way so.

Enter Young Jo Singing.

"Hear de kullered angels holler."

Young Jo. Dar's a big party to-night, hurrah!

Old G. Dar's dat chile, I declar. Wipe away de tears, Jo. Look interestin' like.

Young Jo. Hurrah! white folks go way to morrow. Sing and dance, &c.   [*Exit.*]   [*Music strikes up.*]

Old G. De music's done struck up. I must go 'tend to de supper.   [*Exit.*

Old Jo. And I must go for de bouquet for de supper table.   [*Exit.*

Enter from house, KOOGLAND *and Miss* FLORENCE.

Koog. That house has sorely haunted me, Miss Florence,

Though far away beneath my native skies:
For there I offered love and was refused.

Miss F. To love Miss Chadwell dignifies the lover.
Refusal casts no shadow of dishonor
When honest love's so worthily bestowed.

Koog. Bright hope within my heart this utterance
            kindles
It smooths the way for launching love again.
Miss Florence do not deem it strange that I
Should love a second time   For a long while
This seemed almost impossible.   But now it's true.

Miss F. A second venture will, no doubt, prove more
Successful.

Koog.   You can fully make it so.
Miss Florence you I love.   Start not.   Believe
My declaration ; do not doubt.   Oh, do
Not doubt.   I love, yes truly love.   Accept
This hand once honored as you just now said
By its refusal, and accept it glowing
With all—

Miss F. This is most sudden, give me time
To weigh my thoughts, to balance my decision.

Koog. Ah, do not put me off. The star once set
Let here arise with newly added lustre.

Miss F. Yes, then.

Koog. That word it fills my soul with joy
Kisses her hand.) (*Enter old Jo with bouquet.)*
Now let us go ere absence draws attention. [*Exeunt.*

Old Jo. Well, I declar, dat's just de way I proposed
to granny, 'cept I drew her dis way and kissed her ruby
lips. [*Exit Jo.*
W.)

SCENE 6 — *Room in cottage at Manitou.*

Enter CONWELL *reading letters.—Enter Mrs.* CONWELL.

Con Each evening here bright Spain recalls, and our
Adventures there, the Alhambra and its scenery ;
The time when you adroitly threw the lasso
Around my willing neck, and led me captive
Where'er your fancy or your duty drew you.
This letter says, your bosom friend, Miss Travers,
But now Señora Gomez, will soon be
At Manitou.

Mrs. C. Cease ! husband, cease ! Is't true?

Con. And Señor Gomez too, this very evening.

Mrs. C. Is't really so ?

Con. And Brantley too, comes bronzed
And hale from travel and the burning sun.
The glorious Word to listening eager crowds
He has proclaimed, and now a rest he seeks.

Mrs. C. The memories of Spain will all revive
When they are here. I must prepare for them. [*Exit*

Con. How vividly the past presents itself.
On memory's walls now hang the rolls of time
Like maps unfolded. Brantley's face is there.
The wondrous changes wrought in me I see,
All, all spread out before the mind's clear eye.
And now he swiftly nears my home. For him
I see a sudden turn in life before
Another sun has set. What can it be ?

Enter Mrs. CONWELL.

Mrs. C. The rapid turn of wheels upon the road
I hear. Come, husband, welcome our dear friends.

[*Exeunt*

SCENE 7.—*Garden at* CONWELL'S, *Manitou.*

Enter BRANTLEY *and* CONWELL.

Con.   What success attended you?
Brant. Men hunger for the truth. The creedal husks
No longer satisfy. Communings with
The skies they crave. They seek the joys of angels :
Into the future with longing eyes they peer
To see the golden day, when art and science
In archetypal forms will bless humanity.
The drama, music, poesy, and all
The arts, inversions will repudiate
And live from their divine originals ;
And grand art temples rise to cheer and bless
The race, and beautify the life of men.
Within each temple holy men and women
By sacred rites ordained, shall keep the fane
Of art inviolate ; but far above
The rest will stand the drama's votaries.
From heaven's radiant stage, with starry footlights,
Upon their raptured eyes will flash the dramas
Which angels witness, and the stage become
Thus glorified, the secular true church.
Con. The science of to-day is quite at fault
Ignoring spirit forces and interior laws.
Bran. In reverence let us draw the vail which hides
The world of primal causes, and ascend
To where the archangelic eye beholds
The secret forces, that control effects
In realms of matter. Far above the heavens
In light ineffable, shines forth the Lord
The only wise, eternal. Round this centre
The trinal heavens stand in differing splendors.
Through these to all his planetary orbs
Descends the loving universal Father.
As soul the body fills thus He fills all.
No secret force but finds its source in Him.

From fires of truth divine evolves all matter,
Do emanate all worlds. All orbs through space
"Crystals of thought, conglobing to the view"
From mind eternal issue. Thought 's not lost.
There's nought escapes His consciousness divine
True sight proceeds from inmost to the outward,
From first to ultimates, and thus perceives
The order of unfoldments through creation.
In you and me the interior sight is opened ;
And now we see the angels and their homes.
We see the great designs which love conceives,
And wisdom executes. Our God to know
In Jesus Christ is true philosophy.
This boon to all the race will soon be given.
Then will return the state of paradise ;
With angels men will talk and God with men

Con. You will excuse me Brantley, if I turn
Your thoughts away from these high musings.
'Tis time for us to climb yon towering peak.
I go to see if all is ready now.   [*Exit*

Enter Don GOMEZ.

Good morning, Brantley. Slept you well? I thought
The night was pleasant, and the air quite cool
And bracing. Will you ride, or walk to-day?

Bran. To ride will be my preference. My strength
Soon fails in walking up such panting steeps

CONWELL *hurriedly enters.*

Friend Brantley, Gomez, come, the ladies wait.
                                      [*Exeunt.*

SCENE 8.—*Pike's Peak.*

Enter Young Jo *and* PAT SYMES.—*Young Jo in advance,
sings, "Hear de kullerd angels holler," &c.*

Pat. Symes. Stop you young rooster. You'll scare
away the bears and the lions, so ye will. Do ye mind.
you'r strange to their nose and eyes and by that howling stranger still to their ears. You scrame like young
frogs in stagnant pools when the moon rises. Do ye
mind.

Young Jo. Isn't dis de place to scream, whar you said de eagle flies? I'm young America, Massa Pat.

Symes That's true, boy. So just go ahead a piece, and don't din my ears with your squalling. Do ye mind, Jo, if a bear gives you a tender hug, just call out for old Pat and he'll put the affectionate brute in purgatory quicker than he'll nibble a fresh raspberry. Don't lose the tent pins, Jo   [*Exit Jo, singing.*

Symes. Here I am again in Colorado. The family would have me come. The truth is I talked too much about myself. Do ye mind. The drunkard's taste for whisky hangs to him, and the old race-horse runs when you put him on the race track. Just so the hope of wealth by mining steals over me again. I feel like running away and trying my luck once more. The foolishest thing that ever I did, was to undertake to carry this tent, and put it up for the ladies. If I was in San Juan the day with my pick and shovel I might have discovered a rich mine, and not be as hard on me as this. Do ye mind. But I see them coming. I must trudge on to the camping ground.   [*Exit Symes.*

Enter Mrs. PERCY, *Miss* CHADWELL *and Miss* FLORENCE.

Mrs. P. At this great height the dim horizon widens
To such vast limits, that a human eye
Cannot discern the objets on its rim.
The road is tortuous too, like paths in life.
To heights of truth and purity we rise
By spiral rugged paths, and from each height
Thus strangely gained the vision stretches far,
And helps us know the scope of angel's eyes.
All things on earth are so suggestive now,
Since darkness fled, and o'er my soul now shine
The truths from heaven to chosen seers revealed.

Miss C. The joy that fills our hearts, dear aunt, words
    fail
To tell. Naught can again our faith becloud
As mists do sometimes lowly vales enclose,
And hide our Sun, our loving Father
From inmost consciousness. Miss Florence, you

Have felt this holy bliss, foretold to you
In visions of the night by guardian angels.

Miss F. This very ring with its rich sparkling gem
In duplicate, was brought to me and placed
Right on this finger here, not once, but twice.
A spiritual marriage this foretokened.
The sign is now reality. My heart
Rejoices in the change. All things now speak
Of holiness, of heaven, and God. The spirit laws
That rule us, and control the realms of nature
Unbosom now their long concealed secrets.
The flowers, the birds, the trees, the stars run o'er
With heaven's melodious music, and predict
The glory of the angel's home.

Mrs. P.   I hear
The sound of voices. Tourists, I suppose,
By their approach. Where are our tardy escorts?
They should ere this be here with our repast.

Miss F. I see them coming with slow steps behind
Their burdened beasts, just round the nearest curve.
They'll soon be here.

Enter CONWELL *and wife,* DON GOMEZ *and wife, and*
BRANTLEY.

Con. This walk from where we left our sinewy
    bronchos
Expands and tries our lungs, and strengthens them.

[*All surprised, rush forward and greet Mrs. Percy and
Miss Chadwell. Brantley holds back a little, then
hurries forward.*

Con. Here's one you hardly know; a true, dear friend
Of mine ; your former pastor, Mr. Brantley.

Mrs. P. Mr. Brantley, I am glad to see you here,
And clasp your hands ; an unexpected joy.
My niece ; Miss Florence, our dear, valued friend.

[*Brantley and Miss Chadwell move forward. Rest converse.*

Bran. This meeting quite o'erjoys my spirit.
My heavenly Father's hand has kindly led me
These many years, and taught me my inner self,
And through my love for you has tried and proved me,

My inmost being purified and hallowed.
'Twas hard to bear, but grace divine sustained me.
And now, when hope deferred, had almost died,
He brings us face to face, and may I say,
He joins our hearts and also joins our hands.

   Miss C. My heart and hand are yours. My aunt has changed
The views she once had held concerning you.
Your presence fills her soul with gladness now.

   Bran. Then her consent and blessing let us crave.

   [*They turn and move to Mrs. Percy. Then kneel and join hands. The other gentlemen arrive. All form tableau.*

   Bran. We ask your holy blessing, Madame Percy.

   Mrs. P.

   [*With much emotion.*] May the good Shepherd, who all souls unites
To kindred souls in planetary orbs
Through all immensity ; and e'en in this
Confused world, now sometimes strangely joius,
And by and by will join each child of earth
To its eternal mate ; bless and protect
You both, his tried, his sealed, and chosen children,
Whom, after years of forced separation,
He brings together thus surprisingly,
And crown your wedded life with heavenly joys,
And angel convoys send, to bear you hence,
When life is ended.   [*All sing.*

HOME, SWEET HOME.

The Lord worketh marvels on land and on sea,
My children I'll bless, reads his loving decree.
To the goal right before us, close hidden by vails,
He leads us, tho' care, doubt, or trial assails.
         [*Chorus, Home, Etc.*

No heart, howe'er bruised, no eye streaming with tears,
But heals at his touch, or bright beams with his cheers·
The turns and strange haps that here meet us thro' life,
Are all love against evil within us in strife.
         [*Chorus.*

Those parted asunder, by winds of the fates,
On waves of life's ocean, by Him whoe'er waits
To blend bleeding hearts, do thus wondrously meet
And join in sweet praises at his mercy seat.

[*Chorus.*

In storm and in sunshine his goodness will stand ;
His comforts be given with no stinted hand.
To finally crown us in mansions of love,
He ends our life's journey, then wafts us above.

[*Chorus.*

(*Ring Drop.*)

STAGE DIRECTIONS.

ACT I.

SCENE 1. Handsome Parlor Chamber in 3.
SCENE 2. Part of a Conservatory in 1.
SCENE 3. Garden in 3.

ACT II.

SCENE 1. Interior of Cabin in 3. Rough table and five rough
 stools. Miner's stove. Coffee pot. Tin cups and
 plates at back. Door C. and windows. Present—
 Riley, Harris, Conwell, Bush, Lawson—at table.
SCENE 2. Street scene in Grenada, Spain, in 1.
SCENE 3. Alhambra. Garden by moonlight embraces whole
 stage. Garden wall with C. opening backed by par-
 apet wall. Moonlight. Lake flats in 4 or 5. Vases of
 flowers, Statues, Fountains, Interlacing Trees, etc.

ACT III.

SCENE 1. Priest's Chamber—Gothic—in 4, set with Gothic Furni-
 ture, Altar and Crucifix and Cushion at back R. U. E.
SCENE 2. Street in Denver.
SCENE 3. Handsome C. D. Chamber (4) tables R. and L. and C.
 Covers, Books, Bouquets, etc. Covered chairs.

ACT IV.

SCENE 1. Same as Scene 3, Act 3.
SCENE 2. Street with house, door and window, Madrid.
SCENE 3. Garden and Fountains near Church. Gipsy camp,
 tents. Party seen on one side. Gipsy queen's tent
 in centre.
SCENE 4. Street in Madrid in 1.
SCENE 5. Light C. D. Flats (elegant.) Curtains on C. Doors.
 Handsome set.
SCENE 6. Plain room.
SCENE 7. Garden flats in 1. Snow falling.
SCENE 8. Parlor handsomely furnished.

ACT V.

SCENE 1. Negro cabin. Table, stools, old chairs, etc. Table set
 for a feast.
SCENE 2. Set Conservatory same as Scene 2, Act 1, in 1.
SCENE 3. Same as Scene 1, Act 1.
SCENE 4. Woodland flats in 1.
SCENE 5. House one side, with door opening into Garden and
 window showing dancers, in 4.
SCENE 6. Plain Chamber in 1.
SCENE 7. Garden flats in 2.
SCENE 8. Mountain flats. Rocky pass. Platform set rock and
 return pieces.